Nutmeg Gets Into Trouble

Written by Judith Foxon

Illustrated by Sarah Rawlings

Published by
British Association for Adoption & Fostering
(BAAF)
Saffron House
6-10 Kirby Street
London EC1N 8TS
www.baaf.org.uk

Charity registration 275689

British Library Cataloguing in Publication Data
A catalogue record for this book is available from the British Library

ISBN 1 903699 97 5

Project management by Jo Francis, BAAF
Designed by Nick Rawlings
Printed in Great Britain by The Lavenham Press

BAAF is the leading UK-wide membership organisation for all those concerned with adoption, fostering and child care issues.

Note about the author

Judith Foxon is an adoption worker at the Catholic Children's Society, Nottingham. She is married, with three daughters, two by birth and one who joined them at the age of eight, bringing joy to the family and fuelling Judith's interest in the adoption of older children. The family also brought up a foster daughter, who suffers from ADHD. Judith has many years of experience in preparing families for children of all ages and direct work with children has formed a significant part of her work. Her post-adoption work with children, teenagers and young adults regularly covers issues of loss and contact. Judith is concerned that the degree to which children's early experiences can impede both their social and academic progress in schools is not always fully recognised.

Note about the illustrator

The illustrations in this book have been drawn by Sarah Rawlings. Sarah has also illustrated *Nutmeg Gets Adopted, Nutmeg Gets Cross, Nutmeg Gets A Letter, Nutmeg Gets A Little Help,* and another series of books to use with children, also published by BAAF. Titles include: *Hoping for the Best; Belonging Doesn't Mean Forgetting; Living with a New Family; Feeling Safe; Joining Together* and *Waiting for the Right Home.*

Sarah's illustrations in the Nutmeg series were inspired by originals first drawn by Jessica, a young friend of the author's. Herself adopted, Jessica helped bring the project to life with her charming and colourful illustrations when the project was first piloted. She shared her original illustrations and the ideas behind them with Sarah.

Acknowledgements

Working as a family social worker and later as a fostering support worker, I shared the concerns of colleagues about the degree of "learning disability" which many children in care displayed. Their IQs were within the normal range and yet even when they attended school regularly they continued to struggle academically and sometimes socially. Current research demonstrates how deeply neglect and abuse affect the infant's developing brain. If such children are to reach their full potential they need additional input from their early years onwards. If children feel happy and confident in school they will learn, otherwise their self-esteem suffers even more and they become alienated and a prey to truancy and all the dangers this entails.

With the advent of "inclusion", children from troubled backgrounds are competing for scarce resources with children who have recognised physical or mental disabilities or who have a recognised condition such as autism. At CCS Nottingham I have seen many adoptive parents struggle to get the educational support which their children need. Other children are fortunate and receive appropriate support but they seem few and far between. I should like to acknowledge all those adoptive parents, foster carers, social workers and teachers who are working tirelessly for the recognition of the additional educational needs of children with an early history of neglect and abuse. I owe a debt of gratitude to Dr Danya Glaser for a lecture in Nottingham highlighting current research on the physical effects of neglect on the infant brain and to those, too many to mention, who for many years have been helping us to understand the psychological effects of parental neglect and abuse. If *Nutmeg Gets Into Trouble* can help to raise awareness of the issues for fostered and adopted children in school I shall be very grateful.

I owe thanks to those children and young people who were kind enough to read and comment on this book: Richa, Hannah, Nicole, Sarah, Sam and Joe. I'd also like to thank Sue and Pat Coleman for their "teacher's view" on the text. I'm grateful to Michael Prior, our CCS Education Advisor, for his encouragement. Finally, I should like to thank Sarah Rawlings for her illustrations, which draw children and adults into the story, Hedi Argent for editing the guidelines and Jo Francis from BAAF for her encouragement and support.

Judith Foxon
February 2006

BAAF would like to acknowledge and thank the Lennox Hannay Charitable Trust for their support of this publication.

Nutmeg, his little sister Poppy, and their friend Badge were playing hide and seek in the bluebells on their way home from school. They had great fun but afterwards Poppy looked a bit worried.

"Nutmeg," she said, "I've got to take a photo of myself as a baby into school and I haven't got one. Mummy Holly didn't take any."

Holly was their birth mum but Nutmeg, Poppy and their little brother Hops had left her when they were quite small because she couldn't keep them safe. They had been looked after by foster carers at first, and then they had been adopted by Mummy Fern and Daddy Foxglove.

Nutmeg knew that Poppy didn't want everyone to know she was adopted – just her teacher and special friends. She wanted to be the same as everybody else.

Nutmeg gave her a hug. "Don't worry," he said, "Take the photo our foster mum took on your third birthday. Just say it's your favourite. You don't have to explain why you're not taking a baby photo in." Poppy thought this was a good idea!

The next day at playtime Nutmeg and Badge were playing Tag, when Poppy came over. She was crying. "What's wrong?" Nutmeg asked. Poppy said, "My friend Rosie was sad because her mummy and daddy shouted at each other.

"I gave her a hug and told her all about our birth mummy and daddy fighting. I told her about the time you and Mummy Holly hid upstairs when Daddy Ginger had been drinking nettle beer and how Mummy Holly put me in the wardrobe so he wouldn't hear me crying."

"Rosie didn't believe me. She said I was making it all up and telling fibs. Please tell her it's true." Nutmeg smiled at his sister. "Of course I'll come and tell her!" he said. "But don't be upset, Poppy. Lots of our friends don't know how frightening some mummies and daddies can be!" Nutmeg explained to Rosie that what Poppy had told her was true and everything was OK again.

That evening, on the way home, Poppy was very quiet. "Are you OK?" asked Nutmeg. Poppy said, "After you talked to Rosie, she told some of our other friends and they've been asking me questions all afternoon about Mummy Holly and Daddy Ginger and about being adopted. I don't want to talk about it but I want to stay friends. I don't know what to do."

"Poor Poppy!" Nutmeg gave her a hug. "Just tell your friends it makes you sad to remember and you don't want to talk about it. Tell them we've been adopted for ages and we love Mummy Fern and Daddy Foxglove and they're our mummy and daddy now."

When they got home, Mummy Fern gave Nutmeg and Poppy some pine nut biscuits and blackberry juice, then Poppy played trains with Hops. Nutmeg didn't feel like playing. He was usually a happy little squirrel. He loved his family and he liked his friends, and his teacher was a kind red fox called Miss Spice, but today he felt grumpy.

He'd been in trouble and Miss Spice had been cross with him. Nutmeg went outside and kicked a conker against a tree. "It's not fair!" he thought. "Everything was fine until Dill came to school!"

Dill was a grey squirrel who had just joined the Forest Friends school. He had come to live in a foster family but he was rough and a bully. Yesterday Nutmeg had seen a little black rabbit holding on to the very top of the climbing frame and crying. She was afraid to come down because Dill was standing at the bottom and growling. He told her only grey rabbits were allowed on the climbing frame.

Nutmeg told Dill to leave the rabbit alone but Dill pushed him and they had a fight. Nutmeg won but Miss Spice came and told them both off and they missed playtime. Nutmeg was upset because he liked Miss Spice.

Today Nutmeg saw Dill tease Saffron, a rabbit who wore a brace on his leg to help him walk, and then Dill pushed him over. Saffron got up and walked away but Nutmeg was cross and he and Dill had another fight. This time Miss Spice sent a note home.

Nutmeg didn't want to show Mummy Fern the note. He growled and kicked the conker again, hard! Daddy Foxglove came outside. He put his arm around Nutmeg's shoulder and said, "It's not like you to be grumpy, Nutmeg. What's wrong?" Nutmeg told him about the fight and gave him the note.

Mummy Fern and Daddy Foxglove understood why Nutmeg was cross. They agreed it was wrong that Dill bullied anyone but they said Nutmeg should tell Miss Spice and not fight Dill himself. Nutmeg promised not to fight again. Dill's foster carer had made him promise too and for a while everything was peaceful.

Nutmeg had extra help in school because he found it hard to read. He belonged to the Caterpillar Club and every Wednesday he went to the library with four other little animals to practise reading. When Spike, the hedgehog, tried to read, the words seemed to move about. He wore special glasses to help him to see them better. Sometimes the friends made up a story and their teacher helped them to write it down.

Nutmeg loved the Caterpillar Club and was worried when Dill joined too. Nutmeg tried to work but Dill kept kicking him under the table. When the teacher went out, Dill said to Nutmeg, "You're stupid!" Nutmeg glared at Dill. Then Dill pulled Spike's glasses off. "Spinky, Spiky four eyes!" he shouted.

Just then Miss Spice came back and was very cross! "Dill, calling people names is bullying and it's wrong. We don't do it here. Give Spike his glasses back and say 'Sorry!'" Dill did as he was told but he was grumpy.

After school, Dill waited for Nutmeg. "I heard Poppy say you're adopted! You're only adopted because your mum didn't want you!" he said.

Nutmeg knew this wasn't true. "I've got two mums and two dads and they all love me!" he shouted. "You don't know anything about it!" But he was upset and felt like crying. Badge came up and growled at Dill and he ran off.

Next day the animals made cards for Mother's Day. Dill didn't want to make a card. At home-time he snatched Poppy's card and threw it in a puddle and stamped on it. Poppy had worked hard to make it beautiful for Mummy Fern and she started to cry. She told Nutmeg, who ran after Dill, growling and looking very fierce. They started fighting.

Poppy ran to get Miss Spice. "Dill spoilt my card and Nutmeg ran after him. They're having a fight," she said. "I feel scared. Nutmeg looks fierce, like our birth dad, Ginger." "You were right to come and tell me," said Miss Spice. "I know Nutmeg looks after you, but fighting doesn't make things better." Miss Spice told Dill and Nutmeg off and gave them both a note to take home.

When they got home, Nutmeg and Poppy told Mummy Fern. She hugged them and said, "Dill shouldn't bully anyone, Nutmeg. I'm glad you tried to help but fighting doesn't work because you and Dill get more cross. You frightened Poppy because you reminded her of Daddy Ginger. He used to fight and people got hurt. Poppy was right to get Miss Spice." Nutmeg felt ashamed. He didn't want to be fierce like Daddy Ginger. "Then how can we stop Dill?" he asked.

"Dill's not living with his mummy," said Mummy Fern. "He was angry that everyone was making cards. Do you remember how muddled you got on Mother's Day, when I was your 'new' mummy? You didn't know whether to make a card for me or for Mummy Holly." Nutmeg remembered. He had felt sad. "Daddy and I will talk to Miss Spice," said Mummy Fern. "Dill needs help to be good. Miss Spice will stop him bullying and you and your friends can help too."

Daddy Foxglove said, "Poppy, I know you're sad that your card is spoiled. Why don't we go to the lake tomorrow and find a goose's feather? You can make it into a pen for Mummy Fern." Poppy was pleased. Nutmeg collected lots of soft, downy goose feathers to make a soft cushion for Mummy Fern's rocking chair. Mummy Fern loved her feather pen and new red cushion!

The next day Mummy Fern and Daddy Foxglove met Miss Spice and Nutmeg's headteacher, Mrs Sage. Dill's foster carer came too. He said, "Dill wants to have friends. He's just got into bad habits."

The grown-ups talked about Dill's problem. They agreed that even if Dill was cross, he mustn't hurt other animals. They thought about how to help.

On Monday the Forest Friends school had a big assembly all about fighting and bullying. Mrs Sage told the animals, "Bullying is not allowed anywhere! In this school we are all friends. Each one of you brings special gifts to your class and we're going to think about that."

Back in class, Miss Spice asked Nutmeg and the others to think of two nice things about the person next to them. Nutmeg was sitting next to Dill and he was puzzled. What could he say? Dill was mean!

Nutmeg looked at his teacher and she smiled at him. He thought about Dill being chased by Badge. "Dill can run very fast," he wrote. "He'll be good at playing Tag!" Nutmeg thought of Dill standing by the climbing frame. "Dill's very strong," he wrote. "He could help us carry the book box for Caterpillar Club!"

All the animals felt pleased when their friends said nice things about them. Then Miss Spice told them something special she liked about them too. She told Saffron he was very brave because he didn't get cross if anyone teased him. She told Nutmeg he was very kind and was good at looking after others and said he worked very hard. She told Dill that he was brave too because she'd seen him fall over and hurt himself and he hadn't made a fuss.

After this special day Nutmeg and Badge and their friends let Dill join in their games. No one had ever taught him to be kind but now Dill tried hard because he wanted to be friends. Sometimes he made mistakes but when Saffron had an operation on his leg and used a wheelchair in school, Dill wheeled him outside at playtime and looked after him.

When Dill was mean, Nutmeg and everyone together would say, "Remember, Dill, we're all friends!" Usually Dill would stop and if he didn't they would tell Miss Spice and she would help Dill to calm down and say "Sorry".

Sometimes Nutmeg would help Dill with his homework and they would play Tag. There were no more fights and Nutmeg didn't get into trouble any more!

Nutmeg invited Dill to his birthday party with Badge and his other friends. They had balloons and cakes and made conker shell boats to float in the stream. They played football and had a great time!

Nutmeg Gets Into Trouble

PRACTICE GUIDELINES

By Judith Foxon with Hedi Argent

Published by
British Association for Adoption & Fostering
(BAAF)
Saffron House
6-10 Kirby Street
London EC1N 8TS
www.baaf.org.uk

Charity registration 275689

British Library Cataloguing in Publication Data
A catalogue reference record for this book is available from the
British Library

ISBN 1 903699 97 5

Guidelines written by Judith Foxon
Edited by Hedi Argent
Project management by Jo Francis, BAAF
Designed by Nick Rawlings
Printed in Great Britain by the Lavenham Press (TU)
Trade distribution by Turnaround Publisher Services, Unit 3,
Olympia Trading Estate, Coburg Road, London N22 6TZ

BAAF is the leading UK-wide membership organisation for all those
concerned with adoption, fostering and child care issues.

Introduction

The adopted child in school

From the age of four children spend the majority of their waking hours in school, so it's important that this is a positive experience for them. The impact of teachers and peers upon a child's self-esteem is difficult to overestimate and many adults have vivid memories of a thoughtless word or action – or even a deliberately cruel one – which still provoke strong feelings. Fortunately, others feel life-long gratitude to teachers who inspired them to do their best, and to peers who proved to be loyal friends.

Schools affect our academic progress and our emotional and social growth. Even a child from a secure and nurturing home who has been exposed to books and whose sense of wonder in the world around him has been stimulated, can falter if he feels different from his peer group because of his colour or culture, appearance or disability, or because his peers don't share his love of learning. Some "single" children struggle to find their place in the playground pecking order.

If school can adversely affect children from stable homes, how vulnerable are fostered or adopted children? How does a background of neglect, loss or abuse prepare a child for school?

Neglect, loss and abuse

HEIGHTENED AROUSAL AND SURVIVAL MECHANISMS

Research shows that the brains of infants are structurally changed by their early experiences. An infant who does not experience positive interaction with a caring adult not only fails to develop her full potential but also experiences the world as a hostile place. Her genetic survival mechanisms are on high alert. Add to this the effect of living in a family where you and others are constantly in danger of being harmed – physically or sexually – and, instead of relaxing and reaching out to others in trust, you have to be constantly ready to defend yourself by attacking first or taking control (fight); avoiding interaction with others (flight); becoming paralysed with fear (freeze); or seeking to appease others. These defences are persistent and remain even when a child is in a place of safety.

Observing children from the care system in school, we can see how the over-development of infant survival strategies contributes to problems. Many children feel threatened in the new group situations encountered in school, but a neglected and abused child, feeling responsible for their own safety, will see danger everywhere. Liam is genetically a "fighter", and hits or spits if a child bumps into him. Ruth, an "appeaser", can't make any decision for herself and is the target of bullies. Sian, who has a "flight" instinct, hid under the desk when she started school; whilst Hayley was so terrified she retreated into her inner world and didn't communicate with anyone for several months. If the fear underlying this behaviour isn't tackled early, the behaviour will create a hostile reaction from parents, teachers and peers, thus confirming the child's fears and resulting in the defence behaviour becoming entrenched.

IDENTIFYING AND EXPRESSING FEELINGS

Neglect affects children in other, vital ways. An infant with nurturing parents feels safe and receptive and his survival mechanisms remain passive. When parents return a baby's smile they are rewarding her for reaching out to them, so that she will smile again. When they say, 'Who's a hungry girl, then?' and feed or cuddle her, murmuring 'There, there, it's alright', they are teaching her to identify bodily feelings and emotions and giving her language to express them. By the time she can talk she can tell her parents when she's cross or happy or sad, which is important if they are to help her to regulate her emotions. It's also important if she's to understand other people.

In contrast, a child who is left alone for hours on end has no way of identifying his feelings or bodily sensations. He cannot differentiate between hunger, anxiety or anger and may eat constantly. At school he may be seen as greedy or be tormented about his weight.

Without the language of emotions, children cannot explain their feelings and can only act them out. If strong emotions result in antisocial action, how can the child explain why he behaved in such a way? If, in his confusion, he stays silent, this is seen as provocative, whilst 'I don't know' (the truth) receives the response, 'You must know'. This leads to either 'I don't!', 'You must!' (argument); silence (insolence); or any answer which seems reasonable to the child (lying). When this happens in school a child can quickly earn the label of "troublemaker". What the child really needs is for the responsible adult to identify the emotion behind the behaviour and to suggest an acceptable way of expressing it. That's why therapists and carers working with neglected and traumatised children help them to identify their own feelings and teach them ways of safely expressing them. This is the first step toward empathy, which can in turn lead to trust.

REGULATING EMOTIONS – CONTROLLING BEHAVIOUR

Nurturing parents teach their children to regulate their own emotions and behaviour from early on. Even a baby of six months can learn to "wait" for the bottle she sees her mother preparing. Neglected children rely on others to control their behaviour, and when newly placed in foster or adoptive care the carers' first task is to set clear boundaries until they can teach their children self-control. This can be exhausting for parents and puzzling for children because it's so different from their early experiences, which are their blueprint of how things should be. Maintaining boundaries for such a child in a classroom is difficult, and some schools use a classroom assistant to encourage the child to accept responsibility for her own actions.

UNDERSTANDING OTHERS – EMPATHY

If the neglected child can't identify his own feelings, he can't understand how his behaviour affects others and what they are feeling – it's just not how his brain is programmed yet. Any reaching out to others is done to meet his own needs. This makes relationships with parents, teachers and peers unrewarding and without help he will feel increasingly cut off from, and victimised by, others, which will lower his confidence and make him rely on his survival strategies even more. He will struggle to understand others in the same way that some children with autism do, and need some of the same strategies to help him.

ROLE MODELLING

Children model themselves initially on the adults around them, including a gender bias, which appears very early. Small girls are often accused of being bossy, yet closer inspection reveals a strong similarity with their mother's role of organising the family. It's funny to see two-year-old Sarah approach her twin brother with his hat in one hand and his bottle in the other, saying 'Put your hat on, Matthew, and drink your milk,' and interesting to see Matthew try to match his stride to his father's long step.

The modelling happens in violent families too. "Andrew" was dismissive of females, seeing them as objects of his aggressive or sexual urges, as his step-father had done, whilst Melanie allowed her dinner money to be taken and later became exploited sexually by older boys in school. Both children were helped by school counsellors as well as by their adoptive parents. Whilst it's important for the adults to model calm, inclusive behaviour and to offer children firm guidance, children also need help to understand why they behave as they do, so that they can amend their default reactions.

A strong man who can mirror how to control anger is a great asset, as is giving a child positive goals. Liam's mother had a succession of violent partners and when he boasted of kicking another child in the stomach, he couldn't believe his adoptive father's horror at his action and was deeply hurt. Although this father is a strong athletic man, it is taking Liam a long time to accept there is a real alternative to physical violence.

Each child is different but they all need "rewards" to reinforce their efforts to avoid trouble. These should be small but frequent at first – a child may win several "smiley faces" a day at first in school, or be allowed to take the register to the office, until gradually, as their behaviour improves, the intervals between rewards can be increased. At home they need praise and small rewards – again, star charts are great or favourite sweets or stickers, and sharing fun time with their carer is a great "reward for good behaviour". Eventually, as the child's behaviour improves, it should bear fruit in better relationships with their peers.

SOCIAL CUES

In chaotic, neglectful households, children don't learn normal social rules and boundaries relating to touching, personal space and taking turns in play and in conversation. Danni puts her arms around her new friend's neck and tries to kiss her whilst the friend retreats. It's sad to watch the "dance" as Danni stands too close, so that her friend backs away and the pair progress like this around the playground. Danni's sister, Dee, hogs every conversation. Their adoptive mum helps by role-playing "personal" space and "taking turns"; teachers can help in similar ways, without singling a child out.

LANGUAGE

The child whose parent holds "conversations" with him learns to make eye contact, copies mouth and face movements and sounds, listens and "takes turns", from birth. The parts of his brain responsible for language and reaching out towards others will become well developed.

Generally, a neglected child has poorer listening skills, a limited vocabulary and shorter concentration. The area of his brain dealing with language will be under-developed. This is clearly a serious disability when related to school and such a child will need one-to-one support at times to cope in the classroom.

COMPREHENSION

Some badly neglected children seem to have reasonable vocabularies, yet frequently their carers express concerns about the child's understanding of language. This is often a hidden disability, which only becomes apparent to people with whom the child spends a lot of time. It can be missed in school or misinterpreted as carelessness, laziness or insolence. Tony, aged eleven, could read a page but not understand what he was reading. For instance, he didn't know that a ship was a boat. Because Tony's defence was appeasement, he couldn't say he didn't understand, or remember, because he didn't want to upset anyone, and his school expressed no concern about his development. His adoptive parents struggled to get the help he needed.

Like many neglected children, Tony also had a problem with sequencing which wasn't obvious at first. He could explain the picture story: 'The boy's dinner fell on the floor and the dog ate it', but he couldn't work out why the boy was hungry. In desperation, Tony's adoptive parents asked for a clinical psychologist to assess him. He made several helpful suggestions to them and to Tony's teacher, including asking Tony to repeat instructions to ensure he understood. Problems with sequencing also affected Tony's understanding of maths.

Sadie, aged ten, often did the wrong things in class and was told off for not listening, when in reality she could only remember one instruction at a time. Once the speech therapist had assessed Sadie, her teacher broke instructions down into manageable bits and Sadie did much better.

DEVELOPMENT OF IMAGINATION/WONDER

Young children who are familiar with books, stories and music are likely to have a rich vocabulary, vivid imagination and sense of rhythm by the age of four, and by the age of six will be developing some abstract concepts such as love, truth (as in real or pretend), fairness and courage. They may be interested in space, princesses, knights and dinosaurs. They have a sense of wonder, which makes them eager to learn more, and to communicate.

Children who have had no access to stories, books or music are likely to find dealing with words – in reading and writing and understanding the teacher – more difficult, so many carers make time to introduce deprived children to stories, rhymes and music at an infant level. They can't turn back the clock and resurrect the neural pathways that have died through neglect but they can help to develop new ones in the child's brain.

Such children need extra attention in school. It takes time, effort and patience but regular, friendly stimulation works and to see a sense of wonder awakening in a child is very rewarding. However, when building the foundations of language and ideas, it's important to start slowly with simple things, and not to overload with too rich a diet. Close liaison between parents and school is vital.

FEELING DIFFERENT

Young children may be unaware of many of the above disadvantages, but they will be hurt if other children call them dirty or smelly or if they are the only child left waiting in class because a parent hasn't turned up. Older children will be embarrassed and defensive if their parent turns up drunk, or dread a friend calling round and seeing the filthy state of their home. Children whose parents abuse drugs or alcohol may miss weeks of school at a time unless they have an older sibling who ensures that they get there, so they can fall behind academically and miss out in friendship groups, becoming more isolated. In families where there are no boundaries, children often stay up late and are too tired to concentrate. They are unlikely to have breakfast, and recent research suggests this also affects their concentration, so again the neglected child is at a disadvantage in the school stakes. A child from a family where there is domestic violence may have moved school many times and missed out on the initial building blocks of learning, after which it's difficult to catch up without intensive one-to-one help.

All these circumstances are very stressful for a child and can make them feel school is an alien place. Being open with children about the reasons for any problem and offering to work together on a solution at home and in school can give children the incentive to keep on trying. Karrie was a slow learner from an abusive background who had moved several times. Her adoptive parents were honest about her problems but gave her hope that they could work together to help her. Six years on she still has learning support but is happy and confident in school and is making friends.

Even when a child is living with loving, nurturing adoptive parents or foster carers, the feeling of being different will recur and be compounded by their adopted or fostered status. Often neglected or abused children will feel they have more in common with another child with problems. They feel "the same". Inviting a less troublesome school friend home and encouraging positive interactive play on a regular basis can help a child to feel less different.

SOME CONSEQUENCES OF LOSS ON SCHOOLING

Neglected children start school multiply disadvantaged, but how does loss affect them? We know that children grieve in a different way to adults and that it can take many years for them to process some losses. Many looked after children blame themselves for being removed from their parents and feel guilty and unlovable. These feelings increase each time they have to move from one family to another. They become ultra-sensitive to perceived criticism and over-react in class and in the playground. Such children need a trusted mentor in school to help them through transitions and difficult times, like anniversaries of leaving home, or going into a new class, or having a different teacher.

One stage of grieving is anger, which is particularly present in many looked after children. They hate feeling different, and it isn't fair that their parents didn't look after them or abused them, or that they have had so many moves, so at times they may get angry with other children for being ordinary, especially in school when working on family trees, or discussing their early lives, or getting ready for Mother's Day. Teachers and carers need to be sensitive about these feelings and offer positive strategies for dealing with anger.

SEXUAL ABUSE

Some sexually abused children only realise the enormity of what was done to them when they study sexual development in school and hear other children talking. This reinforces their difference and they often become very angry with their birth parents. It's therefore vital that adoptive parents and foster carers are aware of the issues coming up in the curriculum each half-term which may be sensitive areas for their child. With co-operation between parents and teachers, a child can see videos, or discuss subjects that may provoke a strong reaction, the day before at home, so that his carers can help him with any difficult feelings or questions.

Children who have been sexually abused often become sexualised very early and, despite the emphasis on sex education at school, they are vulnerable to exploitation by older children in and out of school. Parents need to be aware of this and talk frankly with their pre-adolescent child about the danger, giving them strategies for getting out of difficulties without losing face.

Conclusion

Adoptive and foster carers are very aware of how loss, neglect and abuse continue to affect the children they care for. They live in close proximity to them and are close to them emotionally in ways in which their teachers and social workers are not. Even a teacher trained in working with fostered and adopted children (and many are not) will be concentrating on helping a class of thirty children to follow the curriculum. The adopted or fostered child is likely to be one of several with (different) special needs, so it is not surprising if their needs are sometimes overlooked. In secondary school the situation is even more difficult, since a single teacher may meet several hundred children within the course of a week and is unlikely to notice a child who is struggling until the situation becomes critical. Teachers need to be alerted to problems as they arise. For instance, if a child is struggling with homework even when being helped, a note in their homework diary explaining 'Peter is unable to do this homework' should lead to a meeting to explore the problem.

Likewise, the most dedicated social worker spends little time alone with a child and depends on us – the carers – to alert them to any difficulties in school. They can only get resources such as extra one-to-one help, private tuition or referral to a specialist if it is made clear to them, preferably in writing, what problems the child has, with clear examples of the behaviour that is causing concern. A written report for the Looked After Children's Review is an effective way of drawing attention to a problem and ensuring it doesn't get "lost".

Identifying the problem is one thing, and getting appropriate support is another. There is a whole army of professionals who may be able to help – speech therapists (who also deal with comprehension); clinical and educational psychologists; paediatricians (for ADHD and other health problems); play or behaviour therapists, either independent or working for the health service; dyslexia and dyspraxia specialists – the list is endless. Carers need help to find their way around the system, which is why educational advisors working in children's services, in both the public and voluntary sector, are so invaluable. There is also much to be gained from the experiences of other adopters and foster carers. Carers have to be advocates for their children and enlist the support of anyone who can help. Doing this can be time-consuming, at times frustrating, and tiring, and it's important to be realistic about what can be achieved. There is an old prayer, which I feel is very relevant. 'Lord, help us to change the things which need to be changed, accept the things which cannot be changed and give us the wisdom to see the difference.'

Judith Foxon
January 2006

Guide to the text

The following notes can help you to guide a child through this book. It is not suggested that you use all the questions in each section but you may find that some of them will encourage the child to think more about Nutmeg's story.

PAGES 1-3 "Family" work at school

By thinking ahead, adoptive and foster parents can avoid some problems. If Mummy Fern had known about the "family" project, she could have talked to Poppy at home and they could have sorted out a photo together. Photos are important because they hold our memories, and for children who have lost contact with their family of origin they are especially important. If grandparents, nursery or the family centre can't provide photos, great swathes of a child's early life can be lost. Although an adopted child can take in a photo of when they were older, as Poppy does, simply being reminded of the lack of photos can raise strong feelings of loss and consequent "grumpy" behaviour.

If foster and adoptive carers talk to their child's teacher about the curriculum for the next half-term, they can prepare their child in advance for any "sensitive" times, such as discussing "my family" or sex education (a very traumatic issue for many adopted and fostered children). Poppy's teacher knows she is adopted but "forgot", and a discussion with Poppy's parents would have reminded her.

Fortunately, Nutmeg, like many older siblings, has faced the problem before, and is able to advise Poppy and help her to take responsibility for her choice.

You can ask your child:

Which photo of yourself would you take to school?

Do you think Nutmeg had a good idea about the photo?

Confidentiality

Children (and adults) vary enormously in their readiness to share their adopted status and can be very hurt if people break their confidence. Whilst they have a right to expect that teachers and other professionals will respect their privacy, they need to be forewarned that other children and adults may discuss adoption among themselves as something interesting, and ask embarrassing questions. Children need help from parents to decide how to deflect such questions and how much of their story to share before they start school. Nutmeg's advice is a friendly way to stop further questions.

Who knows you're adopted?

Is there anyone else you would like to tell?

Do you think teachers should know when someone is fostered or adopted?

PAGES 4-6 A different story

Situations of substance abuse and violence are everyday experiences for many children like Poppy and Nutmeg, but for the majority of children they are like something from a TV soap opera. It's common too for young children to "embroider" experiences to make them more exciting, so it's not surprising Rosie is sceptical about Poppy's story. It's important that carers help their children to tell their story honestly but without sensation. 'My birth dad drank too much and hit my mum' is brief, but most children would make sense of it. 'My dad broke my mum's nose and dragged her around by her hair' is also true but should be reserved for parents and social workers. Some children may need to share their story with friends, and in this case parents and friends' parents need to work together to help the children.

Why didn't Rosie believe Poppy?

Let's see if we can tell your story together.

What do you want to say to other children?

PAGES 7-10 Bullying and fighting

Dill is frightened at leaving his birth family and joining a foster family and he's worried about fitting in at school. He's probably had some unhappy experiences in his first school and his birth family may have been violent and racist. Now he's going to take control and bully others before they bully him.

Why do you think Dill wants to hurt the other animals?

What would you do if another child tried to hurt you?

Nutmeg's early years were spent trying to protect his birth mother, Holly, and his siblings Poppy and Hops. Now he has nurturing role models in Daddy Foxglove and Mummy Fern and he wades in to rescue the black rabbit. But Dill's behaviour triggers memories of his birth father and provokes an aggressive response in Nutmeg.

Was Nutmeg kind to help the black rabbit?

Why was it clever of Saffron to walk away?

Carers need to establish a good working relationship with the school and ask head teachers in advance what their child should do if he or she is bullied. Especially in the early months, carers need to ask their child directly whether anyone is being unkind. Children may understand hitting as bullying, but be less sure about nasty remarks or being forced to hand over sweets or dinner money.

What are some of the things bullies do?

Carers should prepare their children to defend themselves and others by using peer pressure and alerting parents and teachers rather than by fighting.

When Miss Spice brings the problem to the attention of both sets of parents, Nutmeg's parents are sympathetic to what he was trying to do, which reassures him and helps him to listen when they explain that it's better to tell his teacher than to fight. Simply telling him off would have left him feeling misunderstood and isolated.

Was anyone cross with Nutmeg?

What do you think Nutmeg should have done?

PAGES 11-12 Learning difficulties

There is often good support available in school for children with recognised learning disabilities but, for reasons addressed in part one of these Guidelines, children who have been neglected or abused often have difficulties with learning which go unrecognised. If a child has problems with reading he can quickly lose confidence. Boys are particularly vulnerable because in general girls learn to read earlier. Nutmeg is lucky because Miss Spice has realised that he needs extra help and the school is able to provide it.

Is there something special like a Caterpillar Club in your school?

What do you think Nutmeg will learn in the Caterpillar Club?

Will Dill learn anything?

PAGE 13 Insults

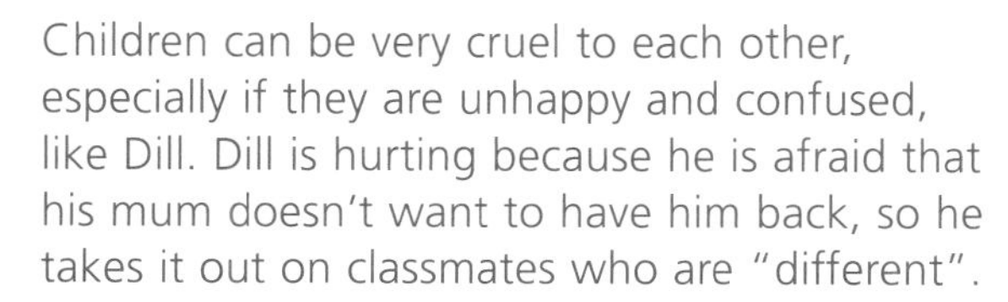

Children can be very cruel to each other, especially if they are unhappy and confused, like Dill. Dill is hurting because he is afraid that his mum doesn't want to have him back, so he takes it out on classmates who are "different".

Does Dill say nasty things?

Nutmeg, who is adopted, and Spike, who wears glasses, are "different". Can you think of anyone who is "different" in your school?

PAGES 14-15 Triggers and trouble

Dill is away from home, and watching his classmates make Mother's Day cards has triggered his loneliness and anger, for which Poppy is an easy target. His foster carer and teacher should both have foreseen this and worked together to help Dill. He needed to be told how much his mum would love to receive a card from him.

Why didn't Dill make a Mother's Day card of his own?

Dill and Nutmeg both revert to aggressive behaviour learnt in their birth family. Dill's trigger is his anger brought on by grief, and Nutmeg's trigger is anger aroused by defending Poppy. If they are to respond to anger less aggressively they need to understand what's happening and be given acceptable ways of dealing with their feelings.

What's the difference between play-fighting and real fighting?

Poppy is frightened when Nutmeg behaves like their birth father and this sends her running to Miss Spice because she trusts adults to help. A less secure child might freeze and stand helplessly by or join in the fight. Just observing violence in the playground or on TV can cause flashbacks and result in nightmares and other disturbed behaviour.

When was Poppy scared?

Most children who have experienced violence don't want to repeat it and yet are frightened that they will. Nutmeg will need reassuring that everyone gets cross sometimes and reminding that he is a kind and gentle squirrel who protects small animals.

Is Nutmeg a gentle squirrel even when he is angry?

What do you think makes people gentle?

Mummy Fern helps Nutmeg to understand that controlling Dill's behaviour is the responsibility of adults. With the culture of not "telling tales", children often put up with bullying for a long time and the issues need addressing firmly. There should be no bad secrets, and bullying is bad.

Do you know what "telling tales" means?

Is it always bad to "tell tales"?

PAGE 16 Making things

Most children are naturally creative. Making a Mother's Day card is not the only way to celebrate the occasion. Daddy Foxglove inspires Poppy and Nutmeg to create original and much appreciated presents.

What could you make for Mother's Day?

Let's think of something Daddy would like for Father's Day.

PAGES 17-21 Tactics

The message from the teachers is clear. 'We're all friends in this school and you, Dill, are part of this school.' It's a bit like saying to children, 'We don't hit, swear or abuse people in this family.'

Do you think the teachers were nice to Dill?

The staff recognise the serious danger of Dill becoming a scapegoat, and the class "bonding" exercise not only makes the children feel better about themselves, it also strengthens their positive views of each other. Hearing his teacher and Nutmeg say good things about him helps Dill to feel part of the group, which is essential if he's to have any positive incentive to change his behaviour.

Can you say two nice things about your friends/ teacher/brother/sister?

Is there anyone you don't like much?

Can you say two nice things about them too?

PAGES 21-23 Belonging

Dill's behaviour didn't improve overnight, but he knew what the rules were and he was beginning to value being included in play. Nutmeg and his friends exerted positive group pressure to make Dill behave well and were confident that Miss Spice would help if he didn't.

What nice things did Dill learn to do?

Do you think he liked being nice?

Is it easy or hard to say "sorry"?

Birthday parties are major events in young schoolchildren's lives. Being included or excluded matters greatly. When Dill is accepted by the group and invited to his first school birthday party, there are no more fights – at least for the time being.

Was Dill happy at Nutmeg's party?

Who do you want to invite for your next birthday?

Let's make a list.

Notes

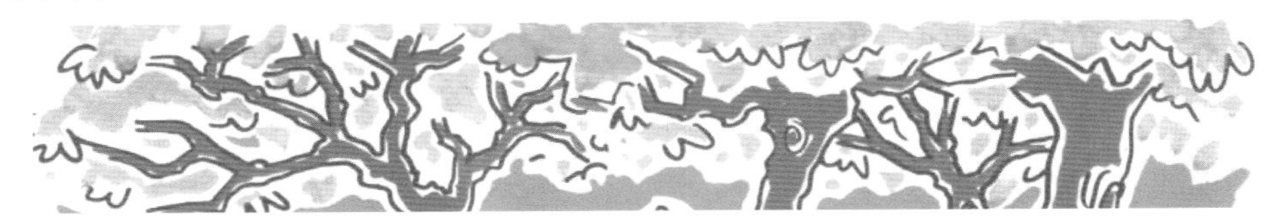

Notes